Chase Learns to Share

Written by: Cousin John
Illustrated by: Catienna Regis

This book is dedicated
to Chase & Kane.

Chase woke up with a smile on his face.

He was going to visit a very special place.

He could barely sleep, thinking about today.

His parents promised to take him to the park to play.

This amazing park was like no other.
Chase could play basketball with his dad, while being cheered on by his mother.

He loved to get on the swings and imagine that he could fly.

But nothing was better than the breeze he felt coming down the giant slide.

They arrived at the park, and Chase was ready to go.

As he got closer to the swings he shouted, "Oh no!"

Chase stopped in his tracks and began to stare.

He couldn't help but notice that there were kids everywhere.

The jungle gym was taken and so were the swings.

All of the children were using Chase's favorite things.

While everyone else had a smile on their face.

Chase wished that he could have his own space.

Chase found a bench and watched the other kids on the court.

"Go play," said Dad. "Basketball is your favorite sport."

Chase explained that he would rather play alone.

Sadly, he asked if they could just go back home.

That's when his dad gave some really good advice.

To make sure that Chase understood, he said it twice.

"These children love the park just as much as you."

"If you learn how to share you can have fun too."

Chase took the advice and walked up to a boy named Jamal.

He politely asked if they could be teammates in basketball.

They played together until the game came to an end.

Jamal said to Chase, "You're pretty cool. We should be friends."

Together the two friends walked over to the jungle gym.

That's where they met the twins, Kevin and Kim.

Chase asked if they could share so that everyone would have a chance to climb.

"Sounds like a great idea," said the twins at the exact same time.

They all took turns, and it was time for a new game.

That's when a boy appeared on a skateboard. His name was Kane.

Chase stared at the skateboard and couldn't help but ask.

"Do you mind sharing with us? That looks like a blast!"

The friends took turns on the skateboard as Kane gave them tips.

They noticed a girl named Jada who was about to have a fit.

"I wanted that toy," she shouted. "It's not fair."

That's when the group of friends decided to show her how to share.

In no time at all the problem was solved.

Jada was having so much fun that she decided to tag along.

Together the friends played soccer and had a race.

They even pretended to be astronauts, exploring outer space.

It was almost time for the children to say goodbye.

But before leaving, they had to get on the giant slide.

They rushed down the slide, laughing with their hands in the air.

Chase was glad he made new friends, and so happy he learned to share.

About the Author

John Butler, known as *Cousin John,* is a Philadelphia native and sports journalist who has turned his passion for writing into a series of children's books, providing valuable lessons to young readers. To learn more about *Cousin John* and new releases, visit ChaseBooks.com